My Broken Vessel

To <u>Everyone</u> I promised to dedicate my first book.

© 2018 R. Motte
Kustantaja: BoD – Books on Demand, Helsinki, Suomi
Valmistaja: BoD – Books on Demand, Norderstedt, Saksa

ISBN: 978-952-339-980-8

Chapter 1.

Why you should **<u>not</u>** read this book

Why – No really; Why am I writing this book? This is the question I asked from myself multiple times before even opening my laptop – Is it because I'm tired of explaining myself to everyone my path accrosses? – Yeah.. It could be one of the reasons I don't deny it, but the main reason was the fact that I have always wanted to become a writer; known author.

For the record; this was not the story I had in mind of telling to anyone – But after spending so many hours behind the screen creating fictional stories after another.. I just realized how stupid I had been. I didn't need to come up with good story. I was the good story by myself – At least I think so.

Still, I suggest you to put this book down immediately. There's no point of risking your precious mind to be confused and affected by me. I am not a regular guy. I'm like an onion; I have layers.. Some of the things I'm going to tell about myself might be disturbing – If you were looking for 'light reading'; this book might not be the best choice.

Chapter 2.

What is wrong with me?

Still here? Ok. Remember, that I warned you.. You are probably curious what is wrong with me. I am too. Doctors can't explain my conditions (yes, condition**s**) to me in English. All I know is that I'm seriously sick – In a good way, my doctor likes to add. What's good on being seriously sick, if you can't be cured? There's only endless suffering until the moment you no longer exist. It's not that all day everyday sucks, but.. Every day at some point.. Your life sucks.

I have something abnormal on – no; **in** – my body.. It makes me feel pain.. Non-stopping pain. There are these **things** under my skin, between the skin, flesh and bones. These things are spread from my neck to my toe; not that it started with that order.. It's like there would be an alien in me. '*Alien*' has taken so much space from me, that it hurts for me to be in my own skin. No matter how many pain killers I'd consume I know the pain would come back because the alien

isn't going to leave. That is why I don't eat heavy medication –
Why would I ruin my organs like that? The alien makes me
have to wear gear-like supports on my arms and legs. The alien
makes me look like an alien.

The other part is.. I have disfunctional heart – I
was born with it. Well.. it's not just the heart to be honest; my
other condition is combination of failure between heart and
brain.. People with this disease usually have the disfunction
located either in the heart or brain only, but I happen to be in
the 'lucky' elite group who has disfunctionality in both of them.

Sometimes my chest hurts really badly with no
obvious reason, sometimes I'm just light-headed and can't think
clearly.. But that's not all there is to it; I can collapse within a
snap not even knowing that I'm doing so: There are no warning
signs – No, I **do not** have epilepsy – . The collapses yet are the
best part of the condition; they last only few seconds and I can't
remember them. It's the aftermath of the collapse that I hate the
most. After the collapse I'm even more messed up than a guy
who you witnessed being on drugs or something like that – Yet
it's just a condition caused by my heart/brain.

Some people acknowledge that I'm not another junkie next to the road when I have collapsed; Even my appearance could fit into that description too – Some people are kind enough to take second look and see that I'm actually having something else going on.. They see the light behind my eyes. I solemnly believe they see *me* asking for help – Thank you all for that.

Most people don't know that while on that stage.. I'm still in there – Trapped inside of myself. It's like real me would be watching really bad, broken TV-program without the ability to change the channel. My doctor didn't believe me at first being able to remember anything at all but I managed to convince him. It makes me unique. Most people – The whole 50 of them, I guess? – don't have the same ability. They just pass out and be out of reach for hours, end of that story. But I'm there and I'm seeing you.

I've lived with the heart problem my whole life.. I'm mostly fine with it. The other disease.. The one that makes it difficult to move and causes me feel pain 24/7.. That's the one I have problems with. Yet; The whole world seems to be more carried away with the heart issue. Trust me – I'm fine. Even there is no guaranteed way for me to maintain my consciousness; I am fine with it.

Chapter 3.

First Notice

I remember that day when I first noticed that there was truly something (more) wrong with my body. For weeks I only felt my body aching. I thought it was just growing pains; for when I had been six years old I had massive growing pains on my legs – So I simply dismissed the aching.

I was just coming back from the recess. I had been playing something with my friends and my right hand felt really sore. I noticed weird lump on it; On the back of my hand. Nowadays I wonder how I didn't notice it before. I showed it, the lump, to my classmate – Let' not tell real names here, alright? To be fair to everyone, OK? – Let's call the classmate.. Mark. First Mark thought the lump was the bone which you can easily see near the wrist. – Someone said that I should tell you the exact name of it, but being all-knowing isn't the way I want to narrate this story – But my lump was on the left side – The bone is one the right, check it yourself. I started to feel unease to myself. I showed the lump to my teacher who sent me to see the nurse, for she thought I had injured myself during the recess. Nurse didn't know what it was, she simply dismissed me. I went home on that day with my siblings and showed the lump to my mother.

I went to the doctor on next week (if I remember it right). Doctor was certain that he knew what it was. Then there were needles for some tests and stuff like that. Well I can tell you know that his assumption was terribly wrong and he did more harm than any good (Doc, if you are reading this I want to let you know that you are forgiven).

Life went on and the weird lump started to spread; creating more lumps. Also, I started to feel the pain grow along with them. Friends began to shun me – For the lumps are easily seen and they grossed people out. Or maybe I was just too much to handle – I wasn't the best company to be around with my constant collapses. Teenage and hormones.. They don't mix up that well with heart problems.

I transformed from a nice kid into something that reminds me of a ghost (I mean.. I can watch my old school photos and I can't find myself from them without help – I look transparent to myself). Every day was endless struggle to survive to the next one. Doctors stopped studying my other condition because my heart disease was so out of hands. I was left wailing my pain of my sore body without anyone caring of it.

Alone. I was left alone with it. I knew there was something wrong with me and the clock was ticking. I felt my body being mutilated by this evil force in me and I was unarmed against it and as much as I hate to admit it – It nearly beat me.

No one took me for real before I told people that the pain was driving me to lose my sanity. Everyone started to listen; My parents, my siblings, my teachers, doctors.. I reminded them about my dismissed notification I had made earlier. I reminded them that there still was no closure in it. I pointed the things they had forgotten to take care of for I needed to know what was wrong with me; I needed help.

Testing started again. People gave me promises of fixing me up. They praised me of how brave I had been for dealing this ***thing*** all by myself – Seriously? I had no choice! I'm not able to leave my body – If I could, I would. On the meantime I went to vocational school with big dreams of my future. Doctors gave me pretty pink (read: **delusional**) promises and all that assured me my plans were ok.. On the second year of vocational school my doctor wanted to meet me.

That day hunts me still. It's one of those moments I think I can't forget no matter how old I get. For some reason I even remember the smell of the office (it was lemon). ”We know what is wrong with you, but we can't cure you – We just **don't know how** to cure you”. I'd still like to know who the 'we' were. There was only one person in the room with me and my mom (I had begged her to stay in the corridor, but she insisted to come to the room to hear the news). That was it. I had this 'cool' condition that doctor said they knew very little about, but I could be a test subject on studying it – Sounds awesome doesn't it? – No it's not: Think about it. You're just doing someone else's homework.

I went through my vocational education with full knowledge that I wouldn't work on the field I had planned for myself. My body just wouldn't last on it. I started to get more collapses again. I think it was because of mild depression. After obtaining the profession I kept one year off. I just couldn't wrap my mind on anything. I thank God (if you have something against Him, that's your issue, for me He is someone who I can talk with without any fear), my family and my friends for helping me getting myself back together. I went to get my second profession. Now, I'm trying my hardest to get a job. It's hard, for people aren't keen on the idea of having someone like me on their payrolls.

Chapter 4.

Family is The Best

I love my family. My weird – Very weird family. Like every normal person I have a father and a mother. I also have six siblings; three brothers and three sisters. For them who likes to be specific, the line goes: Brother, sister, sister, brother, me and my twin sister and brother – There, happy?

I'm not sure how my parents met. All I know is: They have seven years difference between their age, my dad being the older one and they disagree about nearly everything.. Yet they have found the common ground to live in. They seem to have the rare ability to make everything work for them.

My mom told me once that if she would have known that she would ever give birth to a severely sick child.. She wouldn't have gotten any kids at all. **I am the only one who's sick** – I mean, some of my siblings have some severe allergies and stuff like that, but they're not like me. Because of me; my mom questions her own bloodline; She thinks she caused all this. Mom – I know you are reading this.. It is not your fault that I'm like this.

My dad is ok with me. He has stated that even if I'm not the most healthiest son he has.. I have received bright mind and he admires that part in me. He thinks that because of my diseases God gave me something in return. I like the way he thinks, even sometimes I question is it true.

My mom.. Well she is loving, but sometimes overprotective – Especially for me. I'm the one she has been able to take care of the most. When my baby brother died she got depressed.. Condition which she is still fighting against to. She has obtained tendency on obsessive hoarding, which makes my childhood home look a bit like the horrible places you've maybe seen on those tv-shows that tells you about hoarding. It's the mind that's infected; she's trying to cope with the death of her youngest son.

My oldest brother is one of the kindest person I know. He doesn't wish bad for anyone and he acts like I'd be normal. I don't know how he does it – None of us really know. He just acts like there would be nothing abnormal about me; Even when I'm experiencing my bad days.. My brother has a son. We don't see him that often. Mother of the son and my brother broke up before their child was born.

My oldest sister has a family of her own as well; loving husband and three kids. My sister hasn't worked for a decade now, she likes to be a homemaker.. I guess it's ok, even she had good grades and all.. She could have achieved more, but she is happy about her life the way it is and that is what matters.

The second oldest sister is.. Ok, I think. I mean I'm the godfather to both of her kids, girl and a boy, so I guess our relationship is on stable ground, right? Weirdly, I don't know much about her.. I do know a lot of her kids. Her daughter adores me and she wishes to become like me when she grows up – In a healthy way; She wants to have tattoos and 'wrist bands' (my arm supports) and shock dyed hair. She calls me her human-unicorn; Humacorn – Not because I'd have hairstyle that would make you think that way, no. It's because 'I am as rare and unique as the unicorns **are**' – . She simply makes my day. As I have troubles on getting frequent jobs because of my health problems, I have lots of 'free time' on me. I often offer to take care of my sister's kids so she can take some time to herself with her fiancé. It's weird sensation being trusted like that and I thank my sister with all my heart of that trust.

My other older brother. He is.. *Was* the reckless one. He has everything a man can dream of; beautiful house and wife and two sons and a dog. He has it all. That's why he doesn't interact with rest of us, I guess. He doesn't want to remember where he came from after gaining that much by himself. I give him that.. No hard feelings – You build your dream life, we might as well let you live it.

As I said before. My baby brother has passed away. I never had a chance to meet him, he died soon after he was born. We – kids, don't talk about our baby brother when our parents are near. It only makes them feel sad and we don't want to be the ones who are saddening them about it.

Then there is my twin sister. She is my favorite sibling. We need to give her a name, for she will pop up every now and then in my thoughts.. I'll call her Alice, for I have always liked that name. While I have the diseases in my body; She has her own dark thoughts to deal with - It's not up to me to open that topic more than that. Yet; I blame myself for her.. – I don't know what to call it, sorry – . Maybe a brother like me was too much to take in. She has seen me collapsing, shutting down for hours more than anyone.. I bet it was not easy for her to watch me to transform into this person I am today. I mean Alice is the one who has always known me. I guess being human-size angel has a price.

Chapter 5.

Alice

As far as I can remember she has been there. I can't imagine anyone else to take her place – I think it's a twin-thing, I'm not sure. She is like an outer limb for me. Whenever I had one of my collapses she would make her best to take a hold of me to prevent me from hurting myself. She is surprisingly strong girl to match her skinny structure (Yes, I have problems seeing her as a woman even we are both young adults). She can lift average sized man on air and toss him away – I've seen it happen. When I noticed my lump.. She was first one to touch it and tell me how gross it was. She made fun of me for being sick – In a good way.

When Alice moved into other town to study we kept in touch by any ways we could find; We even wrote letters for each others. We would talk and talk for hours on phone, sharing our studies and all. I mean; I know as much of art history than anyone else who would have been in a class studying it.

Then.. Her mind started to shatter and she started to shut me (along with everyone else) out. Her boyfriend at the time told me what was going on; What was happening to Alice (but as I said before, it's not my business to tell it to you that much) and together we started to aid Alice to get help. She is still receiving it, yet the boyfriend has now changed and Alice lives now happily with – if possible, more loving man than the first one; who she rightly deserves.

I can't help to blame myself a bit. It must have been hard on her to deal my problems all her life. When we were at same the school guess who had to explain my collapses to the whole class? – She did. She felt too much responsibility for me at the age where you should be worried about your grades, your clothing.. Not about your brother staying alive.

When my lumps started to spread and my friends started to fade from my life Alice talked me into her friends life. I guess she didn't bare to see me to be alone. I was the creepy half-mute guy hanging with the girls.. I bet most people in our school thought I was gay – Sorry to disappoint you, I was not and I am not gay.

She is doing so much better now.. But I still can remember the moment when I went to visit her and she was all.. Not herself; Lifeless core if you will. It was just so wrong. I refused to leave unless she would talk. For that reason, she got violently angry at me. Some of her shouts still echo in the back of my head. Everything Alice said were reflections of what she had felt over the years; Fear, hatred – All what she had kept within herself. They all just burst out; there was no 'off-button'. Alice had every right to do so; I wish that she would have done it earlier – It can't be healthy to keep those emotions hidden for as long as she did.

Alice.. If you are reading this (I'm sure you are, for I'm giving you a copy of this book) I want you to know that I am sorry for what I have made you go through. If I could; I would take it all back.. I love you sis'.

Chapter 6.

School

I don't remember hating it nor loving it. It was a place you'd go and do your best to survive. I was never the 'popular' guy. I at least don't think so. You'd think that boy who frequently lie on the ground would be some-what popular. No, you will not gain popularity by that. You'll only be that weird kid who frequently collapses and is lying on the ground while teachers screams someone to call ambulance, police and cavalry – Anything.

I have always enjoyed writing. It is what made me feel good and my English teacher always gave me feed back on it, encouraging me to keep going; even when my handwriting started to become sloppy, for I had to learn to write with my left hand after the lump on my right hand started to cause so much pain that I couldn't hold pen on it anymore.

Art was my second favorite school subject. I

could draw the things from the back of my head on to the paper and teacher went crazy (on positive meaning) for my way for *trying* to portray the world the way I saw it. It was hard for the same reason as writing. I am now quite talented; I can write and draw with both of my hands.

I'm not sure how did I manage to do all the things you are supposed to do to graduate from school – But I did it. Next step for me was vocational school for I wanted to get into the career-life as soon as I could. Not what happened, as we know now. When I was studying my first profession and got the depressing news; Most of my teachers were unwilling to take me in on classes; Why would they teach this young man into profession he wouldn't ever do for living? They protested – Good question.. Because it's your job?

On my final year (during the study of first profession) my path crossed with a man who saw the potential in me; He was a substitute teacher, but still. He made me see that there was nothing wrong with me: The fault was on the others for not seeing how hard I tried.

Half of my current life-span has been spent in the seat of a school of some sort. I've been told that I should go back there – As a teacher or an inspirational speaker. I do not rule out the possibilities, even those aren't what I would like to do.. At the moment at least.

On my second study for getting profession I was strongly encouraged to try out everything in order to find myself again. While there, I met a group of most twisted-up individuals who eventually became my friends. They didn't get stuck on my diseases; they were willing to see through all that to see me. They helped me to rebuild myself once again. I reconnected with my faith and enthusiasm on certain things I thought would be lost from me forever.

Chapter 7.

Friends make a Difference

My friends matter to me a lot. Even most of my 'best friends' have been there for me for only four years in a row – I'm not **that** sad about it. I am more (different) than an average guy; So I guess I can't expect normal rules of friendships to apply on me. I do have *friends* thought, from the way back from my childhood. Like Mark, for example. We used to 'hate' each other whenever we had a chance and we kicked ball together on recesses and all. Nowadays we are buddies on social media; He has a dog named after me.. And he was the first one I showed the lump! Yet, he has not been my best friend at any given time.

My first best friend (beside Alice, but I've been told that twin is not counted) was the best friend anyone could ever have. He had asthma and we kind of connected because of that. He had troubles on breathing and I had troubles on keeping my heart functioning right. That was hard connection to beat. After our four years period his family moved to another city and we were unable to keep our friendship running.

Best friend number two came to my life slowly. He was all geeky and nerdy; someone who helped me here and there.. When I think about that friendship now I become sad and angry at myself. I think I was using this friend for getting out of school on time. He got tired of me when I started to get worse. I don't blame him. I must have been awful friend to him.

Next best friend I had the most fun-time with. We were inseparable from each other. Where he went – I went and vice versa. When he went to get his driving license I was the one mans cheering band for him; For we seriously needed some wheels and we both knew I wasn't the one who could make it happen. We went on different schools. I went to get my profession and he stayed on studying some more basics. That world of studies and endless parties made us depart from one another. I was no longer part of his free time, for I was the lame guy who doesn't drink – My medication doesn't mix up well with alcohol, that's all.

Then there's this group of friends I met at my vocational school (part 2.). None of them are my best friends, but **all of them** are my good friends. We have established the state of our friendship to be like that. I haven't talked to them about my insecurities over the matter of having 'best friend'. They are just ok with the system of being friends.

There's 'Kevin'. He's sort of a leader of our group and the one I came across first. He hates me for being sick and he hates the fact that I can't be cured and he once stated (while he was drunk) that if he could fix me by himself, he would, because his little sister has a on-off crush on me, but he doesn't want his little sister to go out with someone like me.. Thanks Kevin. Honesty on it's purest level.. And don't worry; I have no intentions what-so-ever towards 'Kate'. I think of her like she'd be my little sister.

Then there's 'Paul'. He is the quiet one of the group. Now that I think of it, he has never said a word about my conditions. He just goes with the flow. He and Kevin have been friends from the kindergarten age to this day. Paul was the first one of us to put a ring on a girl (Kevin came for close second). I'm going to be a groomsman at his wedding.

Last, but not least; 'Aaron'. He was my partner in most of my school assignments so he kind of just came to the group with me. Aaron is probably the most weirdest guy you could ever meet (Sorry, but you are) – He can spent nearly three days in his apartment without leaving it and play video games.. I'd go insane of that. Still, he is very important to our group. He is like a glue. Whenever we hang out, he's the one who makes sure we all have fun.

We meet once or twice a week (as often as our working schedules and other stuff give in) and do what guys normally do; Play videogames or watch sport or go out to play ball. Sometimes we just hang out in somewhere/someone's place (play with our phones and talk) – Things like that. With them I feel myself like I'm part of the normal society. Best part is that they know that I'm sick. They know it well; for there had been occasions when I had collapsed with them. Yet they are willing to take a risk on having to help me and all that.. And it doesn't bother them. I thank you all for that.

Chapter 8.

Am I Worthy of Anything?

How do you value yourself, if you have difficulties to accept yourself on the way you are? Please, feel free to answer to that; I leave you some space here (Please note that if this isn't your book you shouldn't write anything on it):

____

____

____

____

People point at me every day, naming my flaws. I get that from strangers, and I get that from my family and friends – I understand why. It's normal to be frustrated and I can't blame them on being sick of dealing me.. Yet it does eat me from the inside, the constant bombardment; it doesn't ask permission to do so, it's just what happens – I didn't do this to myself – .

I know that I don't have the '**perfect**' physique for work. You don't have to remind that for me every single day. I know my hands are smaller than guy of my build should have; I know that they're nearly good for nothing – I use them quite often and they are attached to my body; So thanks for being obvious. And last but not least; Yes, I know I look unusual with my huge eyes. It's the medication for my heart that does it, it doesn't mean I'm on high or anything.

Dealing with that on daily basis will surely mess you up – I mean; my self-esteem has been pretty low. When I finally had the guts to ask girl out with me; she never showed up on the date spot. Why? I don't know. For those who want to know; She was someone I met at my vocational school (part 1.). We always seemed to get along and I wanted to pursue something more. Stupid of me, but I guess she could have said no to me when I asked her out so I wouldn't be making her awkward now.

I truly wonder if I'm worthy of anything – Am I worthy to receive any of the things I dream off? I dream off achieving balance with myself, I dream to be accepted the way that I am.. I dream of finding someone to stand by my side – The last one on the list is also the scariest dream of mine.

After been stood up I settled down on studying (which I sometimes regret). Now.. Few years later I've finally achieved that much self-confidence that I'm some-what ok in my skin. I've been dating few girls, but those haven't worked out well.. The blame is on me and I know what is the problem; I'm afraid that I break the girl with all of my problems. People I love and care about end up caring too much about me and that seems to shatter them – I want that to stop. I don't want to break anyone anymore – I don't want to be that person.

I blame myself for causing my family and friends to be constantly worried about me. I also blame myself for shattering other people's lives; I have nightmares because of it.

Because of my guilt I'm unable to connect properly with other people.

Chapter 9.

Never-ending Nightmares

Nightmares of my twin sister are very common to me. They start as a memory of our games or plays from childhood and next thing I know we are in our late teens; fighting over the matter that I ruined her life. I guess I really did that.. Without meaning it to happen. She was the stronger one of us. I solemnly believed she'd make through everything. Alice had the ability to bounce back on her feet whenever someone made her fall. It never crossed my mind that she was dealing even darker thoughts than I had dealt with.

I hate those nightmares. I wish they would stay away, but they wont. I have talked to Alice about them. She wants me to stop blaming myself.. But I can't. I don't know if I ever will.

I also have this other dream.. Nightmare, to be more specific, that I see from time to time. It's about broken television. Plain, old and gray television. Doesn't sound scary, I know, but when I'm asleep it's the scariest thing in the world.

The television is in an empty room.. On the table, by itself. And it shows that snowfall like picture with that crackling sound. No matter how hard I try, television stays on. Sometimes it leaks water, sometimes there's water on the floor and I can't reach the power line because of that. Sometimes there comes programs; I think they might be memories from the times I have collapsed, they might be purely my imagination, I don't know. All I know is that the television is evil. Whenever I see it in my dream I want to wake up – More than anything: I want to wake up.

Dream books advices me that seeing a television reflects on my tendency to watch my life pass by, and the snowfall reflects my inability to see the truth on things. I think it's not the case in here. It's just the meanest television you have ever seen.

I see nightmares very often, I guess I have wild imagination or something. Most of my nightmares end up on my writings as a scene – I'm not wasting any of the stuff my mind comes up with. My dad says God gave me bright mind.. I say He did.. Someone else just twisted it up for me.

Chapter 10.

Home

I am lucky. I have two homes. Not many people can say that, can they? I have my childhood home, the place I grew up and then there's this tiny studio apartment where I live together with two old cats. Please don't judge me for having cats. We can't keep our family pets in a house that could become their tomb, alright?

My childhood home is nice and warm. I remember (with difficulty) when it was clean. So clean you could eat straight from the floor. After my baby brother's death the house started to consume everything; fabrics, tables, chairs, books; lots of books.. Anything you can imagine or can't imagine. Sometimes I wonder how weird human mind is – Why does it make shattered people hoard lifeless things in order to replace someone who once was alive? For me it doesn't make any sense.

The house isn't all cluttered. You can move around in it with ease, but it isn't as clean as normal home would be. I wouldn't want to take a girl to there and all.. Not before cleaning operation – Sorry mom, it's the sad truth – .

My second home is my own apartment. My parents didn't like the fact of me moving on my own but I did it anyway. My siblings talked me over for taking our family cats along with me.. So I did so. The cats drive me nuts, but at least none of us have to worry about them getting killed over fabric – or book avalanche. They are happily fat, and they have dedicated their lives on torturing me as a form of gratitude – They might just be 'homesick', I think.

The apartment works for me as a hide out. It's a place I live, but more importantly where I can take a breath. I don't have to deal about anything with anyone, but it also means that if I collapse I will be on my own. That's why I call my mom twice a day (as minimum), otherwise she (or someone else of my family) will come over to check on me.

One of my neighbors knows all about my

conditions. When I moved into my apartment she came to warn me about having my music too load and all that "This is quiet and nice neighborhood, do you understand?", she said to me. I understood – That was why I moved here. It must have been my outer appearance that confused her. I mean, seeing tattooed guy with blue hair and all might give you the wrong idea of the person.. If you are narrow-minded.

Me along with my oldest brother explained to her, the neighbor, that I wasn't going to cause any trouble. We told her that if she would happen to find me lying unconscious anywhere it wouldn't be because of alcohol or anything like that at all. My mom had a talk with her as well.. I'm not sure how much mom shared things about me (I bet she told everything), but at least I don't have problems with my next-door neighbor. She sometimes comes by to check on me. Mostly on the days when I have hard times getting out of my bed – I try to leave my apartment every day and go for a hike at least. Just to have some sort of schedule, pattern to follow. Almost forgot; thank you 'Mrs. Wright'.

Chapter 11.

The Collapse and it's Aftermath

The scariest part of my heart disease is collapsing and it's aftermath.. Doctors don't know how to prevent them from happening, so I just have to live with the knowledge that any given time I just might black out.

Like I said; The collapse itself lasts for *seconds*; But I'm prone to injure myself while doing it. Worst memories what I have of my collapses and injuries are for example the one where I was coming home from school with a bus and I collapsed before I managed to take a seat. Others thought I had fell asleep, but as I had collapsed I also hit my head violently onto something (I have no idea where and how, but I had a bruise on my head for quite a long time).. When I 'woke up': first thought of mine was that I needed to get out of the bus, so I did, without **anyone** telling me not to. I was able to call home with my cell – Yet I had no idea where I was.. I had skipped only **one** bus stop from my regular route, but I was unable to locate anything familiar for me. I also believe that to be the reason people didn't realize that I had collapsed; I was so close to my home. Good for me Alice came to pick me up from the bus stop with my younger older brother.

But.. Even I hurt myself more often with my collapses.. I'm more afraid of hurting others; When I was at school most people didn't want to walk near me for they were afraid that I would harm **them** – The fear was (and still is) justified; I once collapsed on school stairs and took Alice and her friend down with me.. Along with two other people. Alice hurt her back and leg, her friend's hand got twisted pretty badly, the two other persons got minor bruises.

And that was just the collapsing part!
Let's talk about the other part, the aftermath:

On the aftermath I'm unable to take care of myself for I'm out of reach; I can't read.. Sometimes I can't even remember how to speak. Mostly I just stare blankly while people are trying to figure out how they can help me – Yet there have been few times when I have been able to walk away from the scene where I had collapsed and got myself lost somewhere.

It takes hours for me to come back into my consciousness – To be me again. My family and friends know that main thing for them to remember when I have collapsed is to **stay calm** – For I am still in there, locked up inside of myself. Even I can't remember every detail about it.. At that moment I am very much present, believe it or not – I just can't think clearly at all and my motoric skills are pretty much non-existent.

In case we meet in person and I collapse; Just place me somewhere with my legs up and make sure I don't wonder off somewhere, play me some music to kill time if you like.. I'll come back for you within few hours.

When I had my first collapse with my friends (Kevin, Paul & Aaron) they were shocked; they haven't denied it. We had been out – Walking our way to somewhere (I can't remember where) and I simply just fell down. My friends were clever enough to take my phone and call to my father to ask what they were supposed to do **after** they had positioned me into recovery position.. Which was hard, for my body was still focusing on the last memory I had, which was walking to somewhere – I repeatedly tried to get up from the ground and walk away from them – Claiming that my friends had left me behind and I needed to find them.. Do you have any idea how bad it was for my friends to hear that?

I didn't remember who they were.

After a while my dad came to pick me up. All of that made my friends see that I had not joked about anything; My disease was very real. I've had total of five collapses with them now; nowadays they know what to do – We don't have to call anyone for help, yet they do inform my family about me having the collapse, so they won't freak out when I don't answer to any calls and so on.

Chapter 12.

Sick Workaholic

Working in a real job is something I have always wanted. I planned to work 'til my middle forties and then retire to start writing. Much of my plans are been replaced.. Here I am on my middle twenties, unemployed and writing this.

Meaning of work for me is.. Too much to describe. I just don't have the right words. I'm obsessed on wanting to show that I could be able to do something with a meaning. My first profession was going to guarantee me the ability to live with safety on my mind while I would pursue my dream to become a writer. The second profession.. Well I just studied something that was **supposed to** get me straight on the working field.. Now I'm just trying to get a decent job to get enough money to pay my bills and student loans. It's not easy when you are as sick as me. No matter how good I am on papers, no matter how well I can talk and all.. Employers usually pick the one who's physical health is better than mine or the one who doesn't have tendency on collapsing.

I have worked, thought. I was being recruited last year. I was well-liked, but the place couldn't afford me after six months; much of my misfortune. I still get frequent calls to back them up whenever someone is sick.

I'd like to work for at least five years. Five whole years, that's all I ask for now. I think that people in employment office think that I am insane (I can assure you; **I'm not**). They ask me every now and then why do I want to work; Can't I just face the fact that no one wants to hire me – But someone did hire me.. For six months – Besides there are lots of people out there who just don't want to go to work and there's nothing wrong with their physique!! Seriously, nothing makes me more angry than seeing them complaining about **having to go to work**.. I'd trade my body with them if I only knew how. I'd be more than glad to rip this alien out of me, tear this stupid manufacture-retarded heart out of my chest – For I hate this that much. I hate to be sick.

Why can't some people see that I'd like to be normal?

Chapter 13.

Something Dark and Buried

Like I said before; My second illness almost took the best of me. I don't like to remember these times of my life at all – I really don't.

As you might remember: When the lumps started to spread on my body, creating more pain; I was shunned by my friends and was adopted by Alice and her friends. My body hurt, and no one cared, for I was collapsing more often than ever before, thanks to the teenage hormones. No one seemed to be able to see that there was something else going on too within me.

I was.. Silent; for I was trying my hardest not to scream out of pain and all when I walked on the school isles.. Trying my best not to let anyone see how much there was going inside of me – How much darkness there was wailing in me.

That was the time when dark thoughts came. That's how I call them; dark thoughts. It was them that were talking to me the time I did not speak myself. Fear, Exhaustion and Self-loathing – Together. I remember having these internal talks in my head everyday. The ones that asked me why I just didn't hurt somebody to demonstrate what I was going through for they seemed not to understand it. When I denied myself from that they had a back-up plan: They wanted me to end my suffering.. That's the part I remember with great shame and disgust.

– The thoughts of killing myself –

First I ignored it, but when the pain kept on spreading.. It started to feel more attempting; No more pain, no more days with the fear of collapsing. That's when I called out for help – For the first time.

The dark thoughts paused for a while, for I regained my hope with the new set of tests and all.. But when I heard that I was never going to be fixed; Dark thoughts came back with two new friends: Disappointment and Anger. I felt disappointed for not getting what I wanted; My health. I felt anger for knowing I would never be good enough to do the things I dreamed of.. To do the things society was expecting me to take care of as a man.

Everything shattered in front of me – And inside of me.

People often say that they crossed over to come back to life as a new person. I didn't go that far. I'm not willing to tell what I nearly managed to do to myself. That's just too much to share – I haven't talked about it to none of my family and I will not talk about it to you either.

My moment of turning back to life was more dream-like stage to me. I saw myself weeping on the floor in the middle of nothing. Next thing I knew I was the one weeping – Looking at what I now think that seemed like present version of me, standing there. I asked: – What I should do? – I was too damaged to move on the way that I was, but at the same time there were parts in me that wanted to see more; were willing to believe there was more for me.

I made a deal with myself. The parts that were pulling me down, any anger, depressed thought or anything like that would stay there; In the dream forever. The other part of me would wake up and start living – Start finding positive aspects on life.. Start wearing genuine smile and feel gratitude for existing. That's who I am today; the one who got out of the Dream.

There is more to this story.. Once you've been marked with Darkness, it doesn't give up on you easily – Dark thoughts still come back to me whenever I'm being discouraged – They rise their heads up, but then I remind them what we agreed and they put their heads down.. But that scared and self-hurting person is still in there.. In the back of my head.

Chapter 14.

Mirror games

Since the day I departed from 'Darker-version' of me I had been playing this advanced 'twenty questions' with myself. There's only ten questions, but you get the idea. I do it every morning in front of my bathroom mirror, just to check that's it's still me who's in there.

Here are the questions – And todays answers for your amusement:

1. What day is this?. – Another day
2. Well how are you feeling today? – I'm in pain, but at least I am not Dead.
3. One the scale 1 to 10 how much does it hurt? – Enough.. 5, maybe. I had hard times getting up from the bed today and I double-checked the tube of tooth-paste. Either someone has put glue on it, or this is just one of those days when

normal activity is activity from Olympic-Games for me.

4. So, what are your plans for today? – Laundry day, dentist, hanging out with the guys later.
5. What is the word for today? – Pick any word that comes to your mind first, today my word was 'Hungry'.
6. Did you take your meds? – Yup.
7. How's your chest and head? – No chest pain, no light-headedness – We're good to go.
8. What dream did you have? – I was Huge Gorilla and smashed up my apartment; Most likeable cause for this dream would be the fact that my cats were playing around, and they dropped my stuff from shelf.
9. Are we feeling tired? – More or less.. I think I might be getting the flue.
10. What's the answer to the ultimate question? – 42 (I'm not explaining this)

Chapter 15.

Bite Me

Couldn't help myself with that chapter title, sorry. I'm going to meet my dentist today. It's weird, when you have more than one long-term illness you are been urged to keep your teeth in excellent health. I guess they have a connection or something.

I have never quite understood the fear of dentists. I just don't. They are trying to make your teeth stay healthy. Your teeth are made out of hard substances – That's why they need those weird tools; they can't examine or fix your teeth with cotton pads and butterflies. I'm sorry.. That was rude – Still I wont delete that opinion.

I'm simply going to regular check up; for I have severe allergy over to xylitol and that causes me to have issues with multiple dental care products. There's also minor problems with my bite. I grind my teeth while I sleep; mostly because the pain I'm experiencing – I can't help it. Other than those issues.. My teeth are usually in good shape; I do my very best on that.

My current dentist is nice. My previous dentist was a woman who acted on me like I'd be made out of porcelain. It was annoying. After the retirement of her I was very pleased to meet this new dentist. He is a man who listens to loud music and isn't that engaged in pointless chit-chats – Why can't every dentist be more like him? I mean what is with that weird dentist thing that they try to talk to you when the mouth itself is filled with at least of four different instruments?

Chapter 16.

Pain. How much is Enough?

Second name to this chapter is 'When I have a flue'

Back to this topic. I'm sorry. It's just that I'm having one of those days when I can't even seem to be able to get out of my bed. It's just hurts everywhere. I'm having the flue. **'*Regular, ordinary flue*'**.. Well for me it's far from ordinary. It makes my pain levels rise from frequent 4.5 into 12 (on the scale 1 to 10). The fever makes my heart disfunction even more obvious. I have hard times staying awake and I'm awfully light-headed.

It has always been like this when I get a flue. At the moment I use video-recording of my phone.. – This is what I said to the video – I want to be authentic to all of you who read this. I'm telling you exactly how I feel at this moment. My head is filled with heavy, cloud-like thing that sounds like a hive of bees. My head is red, my chest is red.. I have fever of 103F°, my body is stiff, cause my other disease is boiling itself under my skin.. I think I just realized what boiled eggs are going through – Wow. My disease is mocking me, showing the worse parts of itself. It's only goal at the moment is to drive me to the edge of everything in the existence.. I hope that it happens soon – Now wait.. I think I might be turning into a masochist-of some sort.

The fever has other effects on me too. It makes my body sore; Any movement what-so-ever simply hurts. My other condition hates fever – It has it's own self-defense mechanism; It makes me experience hypothermia in order to cool my body down. My conditions and my body fight over each others wills when I have a flue; My body is trying to heat me up to destroy the virus, my alien tries to cool the body down in order keep everything nice for itself and my heart just.. Tries to keep on running I guess?

I collapsed. It's not unusual for me to collapse when I have a fever. Fever messes up the rhythm of my heart upside down.. My younger older sister came to visit me after I didn't answer to any calls (most of my family members has keys to my apartment). I'm glad she was wise enough to leave her kids with their father – I don't like it when kids see me on aftermath. I don't want to scare them. My sister assumes that I was 'human-vegetable' for nearly three hours.. It felt much longer amount of time for me, to be honest. My sister was so nice that she stayed at my place for as long that I was well enough to take care of myself **by myself**.

Also my parents came by to check on me – I was doing better by then.. I mean I was still at flue and all, but I was able to talk to them. They demanded me to go to see the doctor because of my collapse, but I refused. It's just a flue and it was just another collapse – Two normal things to occur to me.

Yet after having the flue I was hospitalized; for soon after recovering from it (the flue) I woke up in the middle of the night without the ability to breath well. I seriously just woke up knowing that something was wrong. When I realized **what** was wrong with me I called 911 and tried to talk, but nothing understandable came out – Just weird sounds. When paramedics came in I gave them a note to tell them what was wrong with me (On a side-note: I think we should have some kind of service for this kind of happenings.. I mean; Have you ever tried to explain that you can't breath without a voice?). – Oh, I had bronchitis, that's all..

My parents came to the hospital soon after I had been checked in (they are my first-to-call-contacts). Both of them were furious about me not going to hospital with my flue and not taking my conditions seriously – I think I learned my lesson.

Now I'm eating drastic cure of antibiotics. Lucky me.

Chapter 17.

Meds aren't cool

I have love-hate-relationship with my medications. I know they keep me running, but the heart medication slowly destroys my kidneys and my pain medications destroys my liver.. Or that's what the pharmacists once told me.

My heart medication has weird side-affects on me; It makes me have difficulties to express my emotions on my face. Not that I wouldn't still smile and everything, for I have learned over the years how to do it. Other side-affect is that it makes my eyes look huge (the black parts of them are so big that I can barely see the color of my eyes). I need to remind myself to blink more often when I try to look at something so people wouldn't think that I'd be on drugs. I usually show employers a note from my doctor that proves that it's a side-affect – Nothing more.

I don't think I mentioned this earlier this clearly, but I do go on job-interviews frequently. I don't advertise my diseases while I apply on the job, but when on the interview it's kind of hard not to stand out with them.. I mean; Let's face it. I am a guy who wears arm and leg supports most of the day and my eyes just.. Well not that I wouldn't stand out anyway from a mile range with my appearance.

I don't like eating my pain medication. My goal is to take the lowest amount of them as humanly possible – Or just use pain gel. I want to be able to move, to work, but I don't want to be numb. That's what I meant by my pain scale: In hospitals their goal is to keep your pain level in three – You can move, but there's slight pain. My ideal pain level is between four and five. Bit above that I can manage, even it is harder to move.. Anything above seven is awful. Eight means that Hell is about to break, nine means it's too late to go back and ten means Death.

But I can find slight amusement from my meds, believe me or not. It's always fun to hear from young pharmacist how sweet I am for getting my grandma's or grandpa's meds.. That's when I – along with the old pharmacists who know me – start to laugh. ”Those are for me”, I tell them, watching them blush to hot pink color from neck to their forehead, begging forgiveness for the mistake they've just made. I'm mean, I know.

Chapter 18.

My outer appearance

I'm used to been stared at by now. People have stared at me at some point for many years now. First they stared at me when I collapsed.. Then they started to stare at me because of my lumps and when I got my first arm support on my right hand people started to stare at my arm support..

I got sick of it – The seemingly endless circle of unwanted stares. I couldn't make people stop staring at me, so I asked my parents' permission to create something to stare about at me – With my own consent. I got my first tattoo. I'm not going to tell you what have I tattooed on me. I don't want people to replicate me – All I'm telling is that I got tattoos. There are tattoos on my right hand, one on my neck, my left hand has some ink too, there is tattoos on my torso and I have one small tattoo on my left foot..

I also did something to my hair.. To match up with everything else.

My today appearance is my way to give you the permission to stare.

You're welcome.

On my last job assignment, people would first freak out because of me, but they learned to like me. I didn't show off my tattoos; I wore clothes that hid most of them. I don't think that most of my co-workers even know how many tattoos I have. I bet they'd be amazed.

My parents are ok with my outer appearance. They know why I needed to transform it into what it is today. Sometimes I try to make myself believe that I would have probably done these same modifications to myself even if I wouldn't be sick – Sad part is.. I know that's a lie.

Chapter 19.

Bloodlines are relatively fun to play with

As I have a large family, I also have a lot of uncles and aunts, cousins – My parents admit that even they haven't met all of our relatives. It's just impossible, there's just too many of us. I feel like I'd be shunned by most of my own relatives for they have strong belief that there's something wrong with my head. I think they have misunderstood the situation: There's something wrong with the functionality between my head and heart.. Wait, they might be right – There just might be something unnatural going on behind my eyes, I'll give them that.

My mother likes to talk about my diseases to our relatives. That's her ice-breaker on any occasion we go in as a family. I'm the sick son of hers who she has to take care of. – **Mom**, I'm a grown-up man, who occasionally needs some help for I am sick.

Most of my relatives think that my conditions have been created by an outer influence on me.. One of my uncles is a priest. I've came to presumption that he probably thinks I've confessed at least one of the mortal sins and this is my punishment – I'm sorry but I don't recall myself doing anything that hard-core.

I hate to disappoint you all; There is no knowledge what caused all this.

My grandparents from mother's side always acted kindly on me, even when I had my collapses my grandmother would simply do what my parents had advised her to do. My grandfather had epilepsy, so she was used to see seizures happen.

Grandparents from the father's side were bit more stern. I think they had hard times adjusting themselves on the fact that their grandson was sick. They didn't want me to spend too much time with them. Just the birthdays, Christmas-visits and those other mandatory stuffs were ok; Anything more was too much to ask for. I still look up on them; They were just scared of the unknown and did their best to cope with me. They were old, I mean really old.

I have been told that back in their (my grandparents from both sides) days people like me; a new born who suddenly goes all numb, would have been suffocated in the crib and that would have been the end of it – I'm not sure is this true, so don't over-react. I think the people are just trying to mess with me with that story, even I feel there's partial truth behind it. I have been awake during biology classes; Anything weird and abnormal is scary and must be deleted in order of survival of the race, right? – No. We aren't apes.

None of my living relatives have anything even close to my conditions. I mean none of them. Some of them have hinted that I might not be my father's son; For there have been these weird occasions were twins are born from different fathers. **I am** my father's son.. With every part within my body.. The other gossip is that I must have been switched at birth.. No, not true.

I'm part of your suckers bloodline; Deal with it.

Chapter 20.

My Faith

Faith is something I didn't want to talk about in this book, but when I talked with Alice she wanted me to.. So this is for you Alice.

I'm born Christian. Well that's not a surprise, or is it? My 'priest-uncle' was not the one who baptized me (and Alice) incase if you were wondering that. Many people often talk to my parents (disappointedly) about the fact that I didn't reach out to my uncle to ask help with my dark thoughts and all. I'm sorry. I just didn't want to.. I wanted to talk to someone else – That's all. It was not easy to talk about those thoughts to anyone. ***It still isn't***.

When I was a kid someone over talked my mom to drive me into middle of nowhere to meet spiritual healers to help me (yes, we have tried out pretty much everything). I've prayed and confessed everything I can think of to get forgiveness of something I must have done wrong.. It didn't cure me. Don't tell me that I didn't believe enough on it – I'm done with that, thank you.

One of Alice's friends once told us (more likely to Alice, but I was there to hear this as well) about her weird belief of Gods way to speak to her. She'd wake up with clock radio (I really want one of those) and the very first song to play in it was a message from God. That's what she liked to think. Nice thought, I have to give her that. I just don't believe Him to be so direct – Now, why wouldn't he be, you ask. I don't know. I like to think of Him to be more mysterious. He doesn't want to give us straight answers. Or if He does so, why isn't He doing it to me – Or am I too stupid to understand His messages to me? There's also the possibility that He speaks to us in different ways.

I'm not one of those people who goes to church on every Sunday.. I mean; there are Sundays when I'm not even **_here_**. There – I said it, be angry for that if you want to. There are multiple ways to connect with Him as there are several ways to achieve inner peace. As long your way isn't harming anyone it can be the right one, so stop judging ok?

I'm also not one of those people who would preach to you. I believe in free will. If you choose to believe, you are allowed to believe. If you don't want to believe, that's OK by me also. We are created to be different – So let's be different.

When I'd had my 'final' fought with my dark thoughts I seeked out for something to strengthen me against them incase those thoughts would come back once again. I didn't fall on my knees and prayed till some oblivious bliss would shine right at my face. I just came to conclusion that there was someone out there to hear me – That He had been there the whole time, waiting for me to ask some help (I am a person who doesn't like to be helped without my own consent – Ironic, isn't it?). I believe that He was the one to clear my head from self-hurting thoughts and thus I was given the ability to fight against them myself.. I can't explain how I came to that conclusion. Some of you may know what am I talking about, those who don't.. I'm sorry – I don't have the answer you want to hear.

I do pray. I am not ashamed of it. Some days I pray more than once, some days I don't pray at all. At first I felt more or less insane by doing so.. I mean, I had been talking to voices in my head earlier, but this time I was the only one talking – Not knowing at first if anyone would be listening and that was scary.

What I pray for? I pray for strength to deal with my pain. I pray strength for my family to deal with their own hidden burdens. I pray for Him to fix Alice, I pray Him to fix my mom. I pray for Him to wash off the hubris from my youngest older brother.. Stuff like that. – Sometimes I simply tell Him how my day was. He is like my 'imaginary friend' that I am allowed to have.

Chapter 21.

Playing Heroic

I wish I could help out more people, for I feel like I owe it to others, but I know it's unrealistic to do so. I just have to live with that. Still, when I was younger; I made an oath to myself to do anything I can to help others if I see or hear their distress.

Few months back my dad had a stroke. It was just regular family gathering. My dad just.. Went gray and all while his eyes were going round-and-round in his head. It was one of the scariest things I have ever seen; My dad was what we thought to be a healthy man and all. There seemed to be nothing wrong with him. His seizure took all of us with a shock. Most people froze at that moment, but for once I was able to keep my cool and act. I was the one giving CPR to my dad when he went all.. Lifeless. Weirdly, **I** was the one telling people to call 911 – Yes, my arms hurt a lot for my dad is strong build man, but something just clicked in me; That click made me unable to stop pressing his chest.

Paramedics were pleased by my quick actions –
My dad is still alive, and he is doing well. I told my family not
to thank me for what I did. It makes me feel awkward when
they do so. I mean; Have they not been giving me CPR on
'daily basis' from the day one of me? It works on both ways.
My goddaughter sees me as a hero now; She made my sister
buy me a cape.

Two weeks back I was at E.R because of my
bronchitis. I was already checking out from there when this
next happening occurred. There was this older lady with severe
back pain. She plead for help, but nurse kept telling her to
leave to give other people – who had **real** emergencies – some
room. To be fair, I think that no one actually comes to E.R
without an emergency?

Back to the point – I don't know why; I must have
received one of those kind faces that people seek for when
they're facing more than they can tolerate. I mean; I've sat
nearly one third of my current life at hospitals and all and I've

heard more stories and confessions than the average priest on 'a bad Thursday' – The old lady came to me and started crying. She told me how she was going to leave and jump off somewhere high and kill herself for she couldn't handle the pain.

I asked if the situation was really that bad for her. Lady nodded and went to get her coat. I went (run) to the front desk and said with loud voice what the lady had just told me. I asked from the woman behind the desk why they weren't helping her. At this point few gentlemen started to talk to the lady to prevent her from leaving. Some older woman came to aid me to talk the nurses over to take the lady in. Oddly enough, one of them; the nurses, stated that the old lady only threatened to kill herself in order to get in. I don't know was it a trick or not, but when someone says that they're going to take their own life you need to respond to it: It's one of the unwritten rules, if not common-sense logic.

I don't know what happened to the lady after that. I like to think that her back pain was taken care of and she's ok. It's weird; Trying to see how much pain other persons are going through. Some people wail more than others; I wailed in silence for example. I wonder now if that old lady was experiencing different kind of pain in her back for the very first time in her life? Was that what she was so upset about?

I once rescued my classmate (ex-classmate?) from alcohol poisoning. It was our graduating night from vocational school (part.2) and she had taken too many shots.

I was at the 'unofficial-graduating party'; even I don't drink alcohol or anything like that; I was invited. While others were taking shots and goofing around: I tried my best on having fun by dancing, playing and enjoying pizza. I was resting on couch when this classmate-girl of mine started to vomit violently on the dance floor. Me and some other guy went straight to help her; we (well I cleared the way) carried her with few other guys somewhere safe to place her in recovery position without the fear of her being walked over. Those guys vanished after that and I called for ambulance, for I couldn't get the girl to wake up. She was completely out. She was taken to the E.R and later on I heard that she had had alcohol poisoning.

While my goddaughter sees me as a superhero.. I see myself as a person with heart on right place. My parents raised their kids to behave well. It's not rocket-science to do the right decisions. Helping someone is **always** right decision.

Chapter 22.

It's me against all of You

I make people feel uncomfortable when they start to talk to me about their problems. Don't get me wrong, I listen – I listen carefully. When they finish I often turn the table around to tell them what were the positive sides that they may not have noticed while they were focusing only on the negatives.

I think that without my conditions I wouldn't be like this; Person who is willing to believe in the good rather than the bad. Person who chooses to see the learning and ignore the pain – I have grown to be to a person who challenges you to see the good, or the reason in everything. Sometimes others amazement about my emotional strength amazes me as well. Even my body is weak – My mind can go through rocks.

My optimism makes people feel uncomfortable. They can't get their hands on it – How can this guy smile and be happy when his life is like that? – If you'd came to ask me in-person I would say this: "Crying on the ground will lead you nowhere".

I'm not saying that I see everything in pastel-colors – No. Humans just are professionals on complaining. It's what makes people react on you. You have something bad going on and suddenly everyone goes: "Oh Gosh you're now the most interesting person I've ever known!!" You know I'm talking some sense here, right? All I'm trying to do is to stop that mischievous circle. I've been there, in the middle of that circle watching it grow, feeding on people's emotions without my own consent – I know what I'm talking about. That circle is bad, it will only make you sick; **Stay away from it**.

You can talk about bad stuffs in your life; it's normal. But I challenge you to see the reason behind it. I challenge you to see what you may learn from it – Bad things happen to us so that we could appreciate the Good things.

Chapter 23.

Body made of Blood and Bones

I've lived with my body for over twenty years now. I'm an expert with it – So are you with your own body. What have I learned about my body? Blood should be thick, and Bones can be slendy.

Well, my blood levels have never been 'proper' ones. My blood pressure is too low; and ironically my heart medication makes it even lower. I drink lots of coffee and sport drinks in order to raise the values up – That's also the reason why I exercise daily. For those who don't know; low blood pressure causes vertigo and nausea, among other things. I don't want to have any extra seizures – I'm fine without those.. When I collapse there's usually only one *clear* thought in my mind: **"Please don't break your bones!!"** – I try to avoid it to the very last minute that I'm on control. When I do so – break my bones; doctors cry out for help; for there's no easy way they can see what part of me is broken.

My alien is blocking most of the view,

so they just wrap up everything and..

Hope for the best.

– Professionals.

I am very flexible; even nowadays it is hard to demonstrate it because of the lumps – My doctor is not pleased about me being flexible, yet that ability has saved me many times. I haven't violated my bones that much; twice my left wrist, both of my collarbones have been broken twice (different times) and once I was able to break a bone on my left ankle.

First bone I ever broke was my collarbone. I was five years old and it was winter-time. I was sledding down a hill when I collapsed and fell down.. Kid from next door went over me with his sled and that was it, the bone just snapped. Back then.. There was nothing blocking the view, so it was easy to know what was wrong with me.. I should ask that X-ray picture from my doctor. I would frame it on my wall.

Chapter 24.

Everyday Life

I wake up at 6.30 AM every day.. Since I can't recall when. I get out of the bed, make the bed, take my meds, shower up, wash my teeth, eat my breakfast, give food to the grumpy cats and head out of my apartment with a backpack full of stuff and some snack/lunch; Incase I've been called or will be called for work. On weekends I go for a hike in the morning, but during weekdays I like to take the hike during late day.

My everyday life is tricky. For I have very little power within me. I do exercise, but my condition prevents me from growing muscles; there is just no room for them. I'm that slendy looking guy who has icy cold hands and feet, but that's not my point at the moment – Normal activities are hard for me. I have tons of tools, equipment's to help me to do the things that average guy would do without second thought on it.

I have knives which have handles facing upwards, also my cheese cutter is like that. I have colander that I put into the kettles; It helps me to take out potatoes, rice etc. out of the kettle without the fear of injuring myself with hot water. I have one drawer full of different kind of openers, for bottles, jars and cans – I get them as frequent Christmas present. I have also these sponge-like things I put on my pencils to get better grip on them. I have a pill-cutter. I have these special-made scissors what you press to close – I have three pairs of them. During the winter I have those spiky things you can put on your shoes to prevent me from slipping and braking my bones.

What other cool gears I have..? – I have SOS-talisman, which is lying nicely on it's chain. It has paid itself off quite well. I have the arm and leg supports in both arms and legs. They are black (I'd like to have beige ones).

I'd like to get equipment's to aid my ability to write. I can't write for long periods of time; my hands get too sore. I film most of the stuff I want to write with my camera as a vlog – I have one memory card full of my 'Nightmare-diaries'

for example. I use my phone also as a recorder and a notepad.
The method works fine, it's just really slow.

Chapter 25.

You will be there

Paul's bachelor party is coming.. Unavoidably. That also means that his wedding day is near. I'm feeling great levels of anxiety rising in me because of that. Paul is trying his best to talk around her bride to give me permission to sit during the ceremony; for I can't stand still for too long – My heart can't cope well with that.

When my goddaughter was baptized I 'collapsed' with by far the strangest way I can imagine; I had never experienced that before. I was standing in line watching my older sister smiling, listening my uncle talking while people were watching us and taking pictures. Then everything went blurry for me. I couldn't see well, and sounds were suddenly distanced. My head felt like someone would have placed ice on it and it would slowly melt down. I couldn't move at all – I was like a statue; Just standing there.

My oldest sisters husband was filming the entire thing and noticed that there was something wrong with me. I remember people waving their hands in front of me, asking me if I was ok. I couldn't respond – I really wanted to but as I said; I wasn't able to move. People tried to get me to sit down but the movement made me collapse. I was taken to hospital were I was kept under observation for some time. I have the video copy of the event.. I showed it to my doctor who told me that I had experienced a mild case of a shock. Standing still for too long may cause me to fall into a shock – I hate my life.

Paul insists me not to give up on being his groomsman, even if I would have to stand the whole scene. ”You will be there for me!”, he said to me the other day.. I think I try to make a deal with his bride. What if I dye my hair to appear more natural? Can I sit then?

Chapter 26.

Most asked questions

Idea for this chapter came to me the other day at a coffee shop. While trying to buy a cup of coffee I was suddenly being interviewed by the cafeteria worker. All of her questions were the ones I'm so sick and tired to hear; Not that it's her fault for asking them. I understand that people are curious by nature.. But here they are: The answers for the most asked questions of two subjects people can't seem to get tired of.

Being a twin

1. (Whoa!) You're a twin? – Yes. I think I just said that.
2. Are you identical? – No (Seriously, this is **always** the first or the second question).
3. Are you both guys? – No.
4. So, your twin is a girl? – No, she's a moose. Of course, she's a girl if she isn't a guy.

5. Do you look-a-like? – As I said before, I'm a guy, she's a girl.. Figure it out.
6. Which one of you is the older one? – Why do you care? I mean seriously?
7. Can you feel each other's pain? – Thank goodness no. I wouldn't want to hurt Alice like that.
8. Can you hear each other thoughts? – Um.. No.
9. What was it like to grow up with a twin? – What was it like for you to grow up?
10. Can I see a picture of you two? – No. Just no.

Living with my diseases

1. So, you have epilepsy? – No. I don't have epilepsy.
2. If I blink lights at you, will you lose your consciousness? – Like I said, I do not have epilepsy, but yeah I give you that; sometimes external stimulus makes me experience unwanted seizures.. Still, *if* you won't stop blinking that light straight at my face I assure

you that I will only lose my temper.

3. Why can't you tell me your conditions names in English? – Because there are no given names for them in English.

4. If you collapse now.. What should I do? – Um.. How about you call 911? I mean, if you seriously have no clue what to do to unconscious guy in front of you; Making the call would be the smartest thing to start with.

5. What's it like to have those lumps? – It's like the best thing ever happened to me in my whole life! Are you guys brain-dead or something? What do you think it's like to have them? How would you feel about having something like that on you?

6. What's the worst part about being sick? – You'd assume that the answer is feeling pain or the issue of maintaining consciousness, but no. The hardest part for me to tolerate is the limited independence. I have to depend on others almost every day and to be honest I don't like to be the one asking for help all the time.

7. Do you feel pain all the time? – Yes. Sometimes more, sometimes less.

8. How does it feel then, the pain? – Think about it this way.. It's not just the pain I have to deal with. It's also the limited functionality I have because of the thing that causes me to feel it.. Think about yourself standing with your arms and legs spread wide open and then someone would cover you from neck to toe with sticky jam. Then that someone would place anything from the size of.. Let's say everything between head of a pin and a walnut all over your body – Onto that jam.. And then you'd be covered up in plastic wrap. Just add the worst pain you can imagine all over your body and there you go; Me on my **good** day and I didn't even add my heart disease into this scenario.

9. Why are you sick? – No one knows.

10. Can't you just go into a surgery or something? – Now why didn't I think of that? How stupid of me.

11. Will you ever get better? – In Afterlife maybe?

Chapter 27.

Give back

My family has strict policy over voluntary working – It's mandatory to participate. We are all in for it. Giving back to community is a great deal – Has always been. Ever since I was a kid we would attend to various activities; whether it was being a voluntary worker at Christmas party that was kept for homeless people or a fund raise for community center or church – We would – and will be there.

I personally like to attend on community centers activities. Most of the people in there know me well enough now to know that I can't be the one who goes to build something or goes to lift heavy stuff, but I can cook, bake, clean, help to sort clothes to people and do stuff like that. One time I was face-paint artist in an event that raised money in order to renovate local playground – It's now in great shape, I actually like to take my goddaughter there along with her brother.

Voluntary working may not help me to pay my bills; but it does make me feel good about myself.. No matter how little money I have on me; I always have some to give to charity. I was raised to act kindly towards them who have less than me – I'm grateful for that.

Chapter 28.

Art in different forms

Someone said that purpose of art is to create some sort of response in the person who is exposed to that art.. That's at least what I remember my art teacher used to go on and on about. I hope you're experiencing that while reading this book.

While Alice chose her goal to become an artist on the field of making insanely great paintings and all.. I always seemed to have better skills on expressing myself with words. Not that I wouldn't be good at drawing, I'm quite talented on that too, but while it takes half an hour for Alice to draw a portrait of a person I can make it happen in a week with similar result – I'm just saying.

Some of my tattoos I have designed by myself. I literally drew them on my skin and told the tattoo artist to immortalize the drawing on my skin. I don't recommend doing that (or getting any tattoo) unless you are absolutely sure that you want to see that picture the next sixty years or so. My artist knows me from the time I was barely sixteen, so he knows I'm pretty certain with my mind. To answer to some of you who are dying to know: No, I'm not the only one in my family who has tattoos. Most of us have few of them.

Art has always been a way for me to tell people what's going on inside of my head. I can still look at my old pictures from the times I was trapped in my dark place and the pain that I was going through is easily seen. The colors and all show that to you. I wonder why didn't my art teacher say anything to me? Was he not supposed to be the one to know all that? To see all that? I guess he never actually cared.. I guess it was more important to him to get the assignments done without caring to evaluate what the assignment hold within itself.

My English teacher did see the pain behind my writings. Most of my them were filled with violent themes and she often pointed that out to me. I was unable to stop that, and she finally gave up talking about it. I suppose she thought it was just the way I wrote – That I would grow up to be a crime writer or something. I'm sorry. That was not my intention. I was just messed up – Badly. I wish I would have gladden her even once with a paper that would have had a story of happy scenes and all. I was unable to write that. My hands were cursed to write out my torment. I hope this book will clear the table Mrs. K.

Music is an art form that I practice in form of listening nowadays, even some people have complimented my singing voice (I have been caught singing in various occasions; at work, while out with my friends and so on). I'm not planning career with it; collapsing singer might be fun thing to read from entertainment news.. Unless you are the person who they are talking about.

I can also play the piano – fairly well. When my paternal grandfather died people were singing saddening hymns at his memorial service; making my grandmother cry heartbreakingly. Even she had never been that much welcoming to me, I felt bad to see her crying like that. The place had a piano, which was free to use, yet no one had touched it; without second thought I started to play my grandmothers favorite song with it (I did ask the song from my father who was more than happy for the idea of me trying to lighten his mothers mood). My grandmother started to smile and after I finished she actually hugged me (she rarely did that to me). I should probably buy myself a piano or something in order to maintain my skills with it..

As a form of self-help I write or draw something as often as I can. That way I can follow the state of my mind. It does make a slight difference to everything. Maybe someday I'm able to tell what my mind is up to without using tools.

Chapter 29.

Back on work

I was called to work today. People had missed me since the last time. They where however disappointed about my hair; It's dark brown now for a while. I told them why was that – That friend of mine is getting married and I'm supposed to look my best. They think I look my best when my hair looks different – I have to admit that seeing myself with 'normal' hair does make me feel weird too.

I didn't tell my co-workers about me writing this book. I just didn't feel like I'd need to share that information with them.. They do know me well enough to know that I write stuff. I just want to keep the writer me and that other me that works with them apart from one-another.

I love my job, no matter how short periods of time I would be doing it. This gig is only for three days (at least that's what I've been told, but I wouldn't mind that more people would turn sick; it means more money for me). My boss was thrilled when I answered her call this morning. I'm her first-choice option every time and I never let her down for I know if things weren't out of her hands I would still be working in there.

My boss is really kind-hearted, yet she lacks on computer skills – Which usually is shown as late payment of my working effort (something that bothers me a lot).. When she hired me, she saw me as a person. As I had to tell her about my conditions she stated that we would see if those conditions would make it difficult for me to work – She was willing to give me a chance and I will thank her for that rest of my life. Even there were two incidents connected to my conditions while I was at work I was perceived as 'healthy, hard-working guy' – I am sick with epidemic disease **once/twice** a year. Like a normal person.

I found out that people at my old work place have made a plea to get me back to work in there. That warmth my heart. I had no idea they would do such thing. But small action like that makes me feel more welcomed; more valued. I thanked all of them for that on the spot when I saw the paper hanging on the wall. It had quite a lot of names on it already and it hadn't been up there for long.

Some of the folks came over to hug and shake hands with me when they heard that I was present once again. The whole work day was full of hugs and smiles. It was like an re-union; Even it hasn't been that long time since we last met.

No matter how happy I am **at work**.. I'm getting worn-off while trying to apply myself to the permanent job. I'm just.. Getting enough of it; The endless circle of stress, humiliation, explaining.. Why does it have to be this hard? People say that key is to *want it*. You have to *want* the job. The people who said that.. Please be quiet. You obviously have no clue what you are talking about.

I already know that my repayment plan is going to take most of the paycheck. It doesn't matter to me that much. At least I'll have *some* extra money to spend on Paul's wedding present (we're buying it together with Kevin, but still).

Chapter 30.

Paul's wedding

Paul is officially married now and guess who **didn't** have a seizure at the ceremony? I'm very pleased with myself for that. Paul's *wife* didn't allow me to sit (even I colored my hair), but Paul's younger brother and one of the bridesmaids took care of me.

I stood fine during the whole ceremony and after Paul and his wife had left and we had fallowed them down the aisle I was hurried into sitting position 'behind the scenes' where I kept my head between my knees for over ten minutes and after that I had gallon or two of sport drinks to drink. Then I went straight to group photo shoots and all; Without anyone knowing that there had been anything out of ordinary going on at all.

I did feel light-headed during the day, but I managed to work around it. Paul said that I worried over nothing. I wouldn't say that. Next day after the wedding I was on my regular hike and I collapsed on my regular route. I was spotted lying unconscious by two dog owners. I think the seizure just skipped for 'few' hours.. But at least Paul had a nice wedding without me spoiling it for anyone.

Oh, I almost forgot to mention Paul's bachelor party; how rude of me. They were spot on. Kevin had planned them really well, there were our old school friends, Paul's brother and few cousins and about handful of guys I didn't know before.

We had a great time. We made Paul dress up in white suit and tie and he was carried around the city with 'Golden Chair' in order to make everyone see that he was no longer in the market – Or that was the idea of Kevin. The chair actually made Paul feel sick a bit, but he still stayed on it.

Chapter 31.

Light-Headedness

One of my heart disease symptoms is light-headedness. The symptom occurs to me several times a month – Even I have medications and all. I'm not talking about experiencing vertigo or nausea; my light-headedness is deeply linked to the neurological part of my disease.

Sometimes the light-headedness just sneaks up on me. It's awful – I can be doing anything; sitting and writing stuffs, having a dinner, playing with my friends, on my hiking route.. And then it hits me. I just feel like that something is wrong. When I'm feeling light-headed; I become clumsy and I have hard times to talk – It's even hard to think clearly; It's like there would be a cloud inside of my head that's blocking me.

Those symptoms are clear sign that blood circulation in my brain is not running the right way. In fact it's a symptom to inform me that my body is trying to shut itself down.. How should I explain this in a way that makes you understand my point, why this symptom has to be taken seriously? ***My body is trying to kill me*** – There. I don't know any nicer way to say it that clearly.

If I happen to be alone at the point when the symptoms come I call someone immediately for it's dangerous for me to be alone at that point. To be fair it's dangerous to **anyone** to be alone when they're experiencing brain-derived disruption.

What do I do to avoid that all from happening? Well, I have hypersensitivity over to caffeine. I use that sensitivity to my benefit; I drink enormous amount of coffee and energy/sport drinks every day in order to keep me going (I **don't** recommend it!!) – the amount of caffeine and salt from energy/sport drinks helps me to raise my blood pressure.

It's usually the stress or surprising things that beats me; and that's when I'll be found on the floor/ground with legs facing up, eating salt (that stuff tastes so bad by itself, but it's quickest way to boost the blood circulation).

Chapter 32.

Typing fast

I was getting few books for myself from the library and decided to write there as well, for I didn't feel like fighting against my cats over the domination of my work desk.

I was so focused on my writing; adding and deleting, that the sudden voice startled me. ”You type really fast” – simple sentence in silence – . It was said to me by a young woman who stood right next to me. I looked at her and she looked at me. Then she stared at my hands, took a deep breath out of shock before whispering;” Sorry”. ” It's ok”, I told her. She left me alone with impression like she'd been talking to someone who's going to die or something – Or was there something with my voice or impression that drove her away?

I have noticed that sometimes people get me wrong, for my outer appearance does mislead you a bit. I'm not that much sorry for it – It helps me to avoid unwanted confrontations.

After a while the same woman – surprisingly – came back. She had felt awful for leaving like that and she wanted to apologize for it. I of course accepted her apology. It's not that I wouldn't have been treated like that many times before, but this was one of the rare occasions when someone said they were sorry for it.

Instead of asking about my hands.. She wanted to know what I was writing about. She had watched me smirk and pouder a lot while typing. I told her what I was doing – That I was working on my book. She got excited by it and for once in a long time I had a conversation without having to go through my life history of my conditions before we could talk about anything else. She seemed like a really nice person after she crossed the line over her own fear – Those are the hardest battles we have to go through. It's not easy to admit to be afraid of something and then confront it.

Chapter 33.

Changes

”If you could change anything – Anything at all; what would you change in yourself in order to get this position?” – This question from job interviewer has been driving me insane for a week now. ”What?” was my first response, I won't lie. I honestly thought he was joking. He asked again and this time I answered without hesitation: ”Nothing”. The man almost fell off from his chair. He demanded to know why I wouldn't change anything while giving me the most evaluating stare I have ever received. I'm telling you the same I told him at the spot. ”If I need to change something within myself it would be for some other reason than over a job”. – No. I didn't get that job.. Well to be fair, I wouldn't want to work for a company that wants their workers to be that.. Soulless.

Only thing I might change myself is into is to a better person. When I think about it more: I will do anything I can for the people that I love, I would do anything for people I care for – Even change myself into something I would otherwise be not.. But changes need to come within a person's own will to do so; otherwise it's only twist – Distortion of some sort and those wont last.

I will not tell some random interviewer how much I want to be healthy. That's just mean thing to do – Ask something that personal from a person you've just met. What kind of person you need to be if you want to see that kind of pain from others? – Without knowing each other at all you want to open their deepest scars and you think it's ok? Mr. Interviewer, I think you might be sick in some way.. Do you want to change that?

Chapter 34.

Check up

I was at my routine check-up. I do them once a year. It means that I'll be tested in multiple ways. MRI, blood tests, cardiac-films.. All that for **starters**. It's not fun at all, but it's what has to be done.

Blood tests are ok, even I'm not sure why they are being taken. Doctor of course explains it to me in that secret code-language that makes me think that I'm an idiot when I don't get a word what he's saying. Heart films are also fine by me.

But MRI.. My worst nightmare and not just because of my tattoos (tattoos usually contain little bit of metal, MRI and metal don't like each other. So, if you haven't got any tattoos take this on a note: Taking MRI might ruin it), it's because I need to be in the MRI machine from head-to-toe. That is a problem – A big problem nowadays.

My first head-to-toe MRI was taken when I was twelve years old.. It felt like nothing at the time. After the lifecycle which was filled with dark thoughts and all.. (I mean literally half year after it) I went into the machine like any other time.. But as soon as I was completely in it.. I started to scream and cry in panic – 'This is a coffin', my mind was screaming to me.

Naturally, I was taken out of the machine immediately. I was ashamed of my behavior. When however, I got myself calmed down and was able to tell them what happened – what I had felt and why – people became surprisingly supportive over me. I was placed back to the machine and someone, nurse I guess, talked to me the whole time, she even read me the news – But yeah. MRI is not my thing at all. It feels like I'd be stuffed in a coffin. It's white coffin that keeps horrible sounds.

To the results. My heart shows to be the same; even I had the flu, bronchitis, some stress over Paul's wedding and all. Doctor is pleased with my routines and my meal-plans.

The other disease seems to have spread into my back a bit more. Also, my hands are getting worn out by my obsessive writing. I should reduce it. I promised to try.

Chapter 35.

I'm done

Evil omen in the title, my apologies. I'm referring on being done on trying to get a job at the moment. I've been on three job interviews this week.. And at the moment I'm fighting against the urge to hit my head on the wall out of pure frustration. Why they make me feel like I'm the bad guy here? "Why are **you** applying on this job?" Well.. Your advertisement gave me the mental picture that there was an open place? – Who's the idiot here? In every place I went this week I was given straight words, or hidden hints about the facts that I'm not wanted person for the job.. Actually, one of them even told me how naive I am for wanting to work when I could simply go to a disability pension.

Disability pension. I hate that idea. Those words taste sour to me. I am well aware of that I could claim that pension easily.. But I don't want to. For me the word 'Disability' is a curse word. I like to call myself 'physically limited' – I know it's stupid, but it doesn't sound that harsh to my ears than the other option.

Am I turning into Quixote? Am I fighting against windmills here? Should I give in to the will of majority in this case? Is my opinion so weak in here? – Why is it weak and meaningless when it's about my life and my desires?

I feel like I'm about to sink – I really do. My family is worried, and my friends are worried. They know what I've been up to this whole week – How rudely I was treated. They've tried to cheer me up, but I'm just tired of all this. I'm trying to remind myself why am I trying to do this, but now my head is empty from the reasons – I can't relate to my own words, that's how mad I am at the moment and that's bad.

I think I need some time out.

Chapter 36.

Remote Yourself

Even the next chapter ended up on me stating that I needed a break – I didn't went on doing so. I channeled my frustration into the chapters 13 and 38 (naturally, I made vlogs which I later on typed clean). After those I felt calmed enough to do something else.

I have always liked travelling. I have been once abroad; just once. It was a school trip for a week and it took insanely a lot reassurance from me to convince my parents to allow me to join in it – My teachers didn't first believe that my parents actually gave their consent; they called my parents to check it up (I was standing in front of a bus while one of the teachers went to call my parents from the office to confirm that I didn't forge their signatures).

When I was a kid we used to travel a lot as a family. I liked those trips a lot. Still, when my heart disease went out of hands it all ended. I felt bad for that. I begged my parents not to do that to my brothers and sisters, I didn't want them to be punished for my health issues – It was useless fight.. I guess my medical bills were partial reason for their decision. My dad tried occasionally to cheer us with small road trips. It was the best he could offer, and I thank him for that.

If I could pass the required health check that is related to the driving license I would make road trips as much as possible; That much I learned to like them. Surprisingly, I do know how to drive a car (you don't need a piece of paper for that). I really do – My dad thought me how to drive; for we both figured that it could be a skill I could need in emergency situations.

Kevin, Paul, Aaron and I are planning to make some kind of trip together on next summer. I guess Paul's wife and Kevin's bride will be joining us. We haven't talked about the details of the trip yet for we are still trying to figure out *when* the trip will take it's place. I haven't talked to my family about this trip – I don't want them to start worry over nothing. My boys and I are well-aware of the risk of me participating to this trip. Yet, I think I'm the last person to be worried about on it; Me, Kevin and Paul have no idea what might happen if Aaron isn't able to play his video games..

To the point of the chapter. There is this one place I like to go when I'm feeling down. I can go there all by myself. It' a place I go to clear my head ; Sometimes you need to go out of frames and I have learned over the years to remote myself from everything time to times.. I do that in order to cool myself down and to silence the discouraging whispers from the back of my head – To be able to listen myself.

From there, the remote place of mine.. Everything seems so small and void. It makes me able to remember the fact that no matter what worries I think I have.. Most of them are just illusion made up by society. Your only worries should be about caring your loved ones and having food in your fridge.

Chapter 37.

Back at the Library

I was at the library again. She came to me again, the woman I talked last time. She wanted to know how my book was coming up. "Slowly", I admitted. She was there with a friend this time to return her books. Her friend intervened us that much that she made me gave my number to them – more likely to the woman I know from my earlier session from library.

After a day she texted me. I responded and we started to talk some more.. We did go on a date few days ago. There's something within her that makes me feel different about myself. I'm not sure yet is it good or bad difference; I hope it's good.

She did ask about my hands this time – But she asked gently, not wanting to hurt my feelings. Her reaction was.. Priceless. While on our first encounter with each other's she nearly run away for being scared – This time she wanted to actually take a look at my hand to see what was on (or **in**, I can't decide) it.

So, there we were. Staring at my unsupported hand; me watching her tracing the lumps on it. She was very calm. She stated that she had expected it to look far worse; that my hand would be full of scars and everything. I don't think that I've ever heard anyone expecting to see that of me – Not that everyone would have told me what they think is under my arm supports. The way she thinks about things is refreshing and unique. I like that about her. Do you know the types of persons who seem to be able to affect on time? I know about handful of those and weirdly; She can do that – Time stops and goes fast forward at the same time when I'm with her. It's confusing in a way that doesn't scare me; it lures me.

I don't know where this is going to. I'm not going to paint any pretty pictures in here. It's already disturbing that I mention her to all of you. She will most likely read all of this.

All I know is that I'd like to meet her again.

Chapter 38.

Darkness attracts Madness

I have gone a long way from the days were my will to live was almost non-existent.. My dark thoughts almost made me commit suicide – There, I finally wrote that word.

I am marked by those events. All of those thoughts and acts attracted that much Madness in me that it would be dishonest to say that there wouldn't be any traces of it left – Remaining's of it lives in the back of my head in form of great levels of anxiety and guilt; Which I continue to work on. Even the marks are not visible, they do exist.

My family and closest friends do know about my dark thoughts and all – Even I have never talked about the details of them. Those are the things that I keep as my own – Something Hidden and Buried within me. There is no point of hurting others by telling more than there is needed to know: I was in a dark place, I was going to do something irretrievably stupid to myself, I didn't and got help – Out of concept; That's the shortest story I have ever told anyone.

Once a person I know came to say to me that I was too coward to go through with my attempt to take my own life (Yes, that person had guts to call me a coward over that). Other people who over heard this person were ready to defend me; they were shouting how rude it was to say something like that and some of my friends were ready to pin that person on the wall.. I was stunned by the words. Still; I thanked the person for the honest opinion given to me. I'm well trained in good manners and therefore I was unable to let myself sink into same level – To respond into something that cold and cruel with similar way.

I know that what the person said to me is not true at all. I am not a coward – It was way braver act from me to fight against my own twisted mind. I'm well aware that my 'dark thoughts' are terrifying; They are strong enough to scare out people who they shouldn't be even able to reach – Because the thoughts were inside of *my* head and are currently non-existent. Oddly they can somehow still affect on people and make them believe that it's wrong of me to stand here. If fighting against something that strong makes me a coward.. What are the people who call me a coward then? – They haven't faced *my* 'dark thoughts' personally, yet they are ready to send me to my death – Not willing to even meet one personification of my darkness by themselves.. Just saying.

For the record; I have never been declared to have lost my sanity, but I believe that I wasn't that far from that; for when everything shattered for me.. I was in pieces in every aspect you can imagine – I was a hollow wreck that only resembled a human. Slowly.. I was filled with something to keep me together. It was something close to a tar; emotionally poisonous tar that made me unable to see things in the right way. It made me believe that my death would make people who loved and cared about me *happy* – They wouldn't have to worry about me no longer.

I'm telling you something that might save you some day:

People who care and love you won't be thinking that you are a
burden,
that you are something 'they need to worry about'.
Their love for you is not to be read as 'worry'.
The most cruelest thing you can do to others is to deny them
the right of loving you..

To stop existing.

...

I recently realized that in my dream-like state all those years
ago..
I wasn't just confronted by My Will to Live

...

I found something.

Something strong and unused..

–   I found Light within me to thwart most of the Darkness
away –

Chapter 39.

My Vessel

Vessel – noun.

Word that is used to describe an empty instrument / utensil.

It's not the vessel itself that is important; it's what it contains that makes it important. Human body is often considered to be the Vessel of the Soul. Vessel is what protects the Soul from outer harm.

Nothing in Life is created without a purpose; My vessel is no exception. My vessel is broken. It has always been, it always will be – There is no denial on that fact. All I know for sure is.. This vessel might be broken, but it's not meaningless. I give meaning to it. I'm the one that gives it a reason to exist; I fill it. The fractures of my vessel may determine the majority of my life, but it doesn't have to make **Me** be superseded. I need to learn how to avoid that.

Even my Soul is not completely covered –
Someone knew I was strong enough to handle my vessel the
way it was. My Soul is still intact, even it has been tainted. I
guess some battles can not been won without scars.

No one has ever promised us that living would be
easy. My life for example is one irrational rollercoaster ride and
I'm (still) learning how to take matters into my own hands –
Aren't we all trying to accomplish that?

I don't know how or why.. But day after a day I'm
starting to appreciate all that I've received. Maybe writing of
this book has helped on it, who knows for sure? My final
conclusion of my situation is that my life might not be what I
wanted – It's what I needed.

I'm going to see this through – That's the promise I made to
myself.

About 'My Broken Vessel'

This book is my first published novel. It's based on real events of my own life; Yet parts of it are purely made up by my imagination, Any familiarity with real persons and places are unintentional.

Even this book started out as a project to give myself a voice.. I want to use that voice to all of us in similar situations: I hope that this book has opened your eyes to all of us who usually hide in the shadows, for we are been shunned or discouraged by most of you with our differences.. Not all of us get to choose what we are given.

I will continue writing, I think I have finally found the tone I was searching for so many years.. I have to warn you, that there might not be sequel to this book – Or then there will be one, I don't know. Life is tricky; sometimes so disappointing – yet sometimes very surprising thing.

Last, but not least:

Thank you for reading my story.

I'd also like to thank..

- I would like to thank my loving and super-supportive family (Sorry if some of you seemed like bad guys – They really are not!!). You are the best, no matter what.. Mom, I still love you and I will call you every day. Dad, thanks for always knowing what to say to get me back to my feet. My siblings; You know I love you. Thank you for being there.
- My friends, the tiny group of you; Thank you. Even I'm not the best company, you always make time for me and you make me feel normal. It means the World to me.
- My teachers along the way; You told me not to give up – I didn't and here I am.
- All the other people that I didn't mention already; Thank you.